# Pi____
# Paint for
# a Pixie

illustrated by
Colin & Moira Maclean

AWARD PUBLICATIONS LIMITED

Once, when Linda was playing at the bottom of her garden, she heard a funny noise. She stopped and listened.

'If a bird could speak, it would speak just like that funny voice,' thought Linda, in surprise. 'It *is* somebody talking – it's a very small voice, high and clear.'

She sat perfectly still, listening, trying to hear what the voice said.

'Just my luck!' said the voice. 'Finished the tea-set all but three cups – and now I've run out of paint. Isn't that just my luck?'

Linda quietly popped her head through a gap in the hedge to see who could be talking. It didn't sound at all like a child. It wasn't a child, either.

'It's a pixie!' said Linda, in the greatest surprise. 'Well, who would have thought I'd ever see a pixie! I've looked for years and years and never seen one. But this *must* be one – and he's talking to himself. What is he doing?'

She looked closely and saw that he was painting a very small tea-set, just big enough for him to drink from. The cups

and saucers were about the size of the
ones in Linda's doll's house.

Suddenly the tiny fellow heard Linda
breathing and he looked up. He stared in
surprise at the little girl's head peeping
through the hedge.

# PINK PAINT FOR A PIXIE

'Hello!' he said. 'Isn't it a nuisance – I've run out of pink paint.'

'What are you doing?' asked Linda.

'I'm painting a pretty pattern on these cups,' said the pixie, and he held one up for Linda to see.

He certainly was putting a very pretty pattern on each one. There were pink roses and green leaves all the way round. The saucers and plates had the same pattern.

Linda looked at the tiny tubes of paint beside the pixie. The tube of pink paint was squeezed quite empty.

'Can't you finish your work?' she asked.

'No,' said the pixie. 'And I promised the Princess Peronel she should have the whole set tomorrow, for her birthday party. It's really annoying.'

Linda suddenly had a splendid idea. *She* had some tubes of paint in her

paint-box. One might be pink. If so, she could lend it to the pixie!

'I believe I could help you,' she said. 'I've got some paints. I'll go and get the tube of pink. Wait here a minute.' She ran indoors and found her paint-box.

## PINK PAINT FOR A PIXIE

'Darling, surely you are not going to paint indoors this fine morning!' said her mother when she saw Linda getting out her paint-box.

'No, Mummy – I'm lending a tube of pink paint to a pixie,' said Linda.

Her mother laughed. 'What funny things you do say, Linda!' she said. She didn't guess for a minute that Linda was speaking the truth. She thought she was just pretending.

Linda ran out again, holding in her hand a tube of crimson paint. She knew that if the pixie mixed the deep red with water, the colour would be pink. She was soon back at the hedge again.

'Here you are,' she said. 'I'm sure this will make a lovely pink.'

'You *are* a good friend!' said the pixie,

gratefully. 'You can watch me paint if you like.'

Linda sat and watched him. He had a tiny china palette on which he mixed his colours. He squeezed some of the crimson out on to it, and then dipped his tiny brush into a dewdrop hanging on a grass nearby. Soon he had just the right pink for the little cups. It was fun to watch him painting roses round the cup he was holding.

# PINK PAINT FOR A PIXIE

'I don't know what I should have done if you hadn't helped me,' he said. 'Can I do anything for you in return?'

'I suppose you couldn't make a wish come true, could you?' asked Linda, at once. The pixie shook his head.

'No,' he said. 'I don't know powerful enough magic for that. If I did I'd have wished for a new tube of pink paint for myself. But if you really want a wish to come true why don't you find a four-leaved clover, put it under your pillow, and wish before you go to sleep?'

'There aren't any four-leaved clovers round about here,' said Linda. 'The other children and I have looked and looked, but we have never found one.'

'Well, go to where the foxgloves grow, pick up a fallen foxglove bell, slip it on your thumb and wish,' said the pixie.

'The foxgloves aren't out yet,' said Linda.

'Of course they aren't!' said the pixie. 'How silly of me. Well, try the pink-tipped daisy spell, then.'

# PINK PAINT FOR A PIXIE

'What's that?' asked Linda.

'You pick thirteen pink-tipped daisies,' said the pixie. 'You make them into a daisy-chain, and wear them round your neck for one hour at four o'clock in the daytime. You wish your wish thirteen

times in that hour. Then you take off the chain and put the daisies in water. You mustn't forget to do that, because if you don't give them a drink, the magic won't work.'

'That sounds a good spell,' said Linda. 'But there aren't any pink-tipped daisies round here, pixie. Look – they are quite white.'

The little girl picked two or three daisies and showed them to the pixie. He looked underneath the petals at the very tips. He shook his head.

'You're right,' he said. 'Not a pink tip to be seen. Very tiresome. Well, I must think of something else for you.'

A bell rang in the distance. Linda got up. 'That's for my dinner,' she said. 'I must go. I'll come back again afterwards.'

'I'll think of something whilst you are gone,' said the pixie. He thought and he thought. But he could think of no other way of making a wish come true. He was only a small pixie, not very old, and he really didn't know a great deal of magic.

# PINK PAINT FOR A PIXIE

Then a fine idea came into his small head. Hadn't he got plenty of pink paint in that tube? Well, why shouldn't he paint all the daisies round about with pink tips?

'Good idea!' he said, and as soon as he finished his tea-set, he went to the daisies, sat underneath the little flowers,

and carefully ran his brush, full of pink paint, under the tip of each petal. Soon the first daisy looked really pretty. It turned up its petals a little to show the pink underneath.

'I hope Linda comes back soon,' thought the pixie. 'Then I can tell her what I've done.'

## PINK PAINT FOR A PIXIE

But Linda didn't come back. Her mother had said she must have a rest after dinner, and the little girl was in her bed, hoping that the pixie would still be in the field when she got up at three o'clock.

He wasn't. He had packed up his painted tea-set for the Princess Peronel and gone. But there were the daisies, all pink-tipped! And there was the little tube of paint left beside them, half-empty now, with the top put neatly on.

Linda looked round for the pixie when she crept out through the hedge into the field after her rest. He wasn't there. But there was her tube of paint – and, oh, what a surprise, it was lying by a daisy-plant, where five pink-tipped daisies

grew together, their golden eyes looking
straight at Linda!

'He's painted your tips pink! The
underneaths of your pretty white petals
are crimson pink! Now I can try that
magic spell!'

Linda picked thirteen daisies and made them into a chain. You know how she made it, don't you? She slit each stalk near its end with a pin, and then slipped a daisy through the slit, so that soon the thirteen were hanging in a pretty chain. She joined the chain – and looked at her watch.

'Four o'clock! Now I'll wear it – and before five o'clock I will wish my wish thirteen times!'

# PINK PAINT FOR A PIXIE

She wore the daisy-chain, and wished
her wish thirteen times in the hour. Then
she took off the chain and put the daisies
into water to have a drink. She wished for
her big soldier-brother to come back from
far away – and, will you believe it, he
came home the very next day. She rushed
out to tell the pixie, but she has never
seen him again.

Have you seen pink-tipped daisies? Go
out and look for some; maybe you will
find thirteen!

For further information on Enid Blyton please contact www.blyton.com

ISBN 0-86163-709-7

Text copyright The Enid Blyton Company
Illustrations copyright © 1998 Award Publications Limited

Enid Blyton's signature is a trademark of The Enid Blyton Company

First published in *A Story Party at Green Hedges*

This edition first published 1998 by Award Publications Limited,
27 Longford Street, London NW1 3DZ

Printed in India